A Christian Journey
Chloe's Missing Piece

By Wanda Rawlings

A Christian Journey
Chloe's Missing Piece

ISBN: 978-1-959702-16-0
Copyright ©2023 Wanda Rawlings

Library of Congress Cataloging-in-Publication Data

All rights reserved solely by the author. The author guarantees all contents are original and do not infringe upon the legal rights of any other person or work. No part of this book may be reproduced, shared in a retrieval system, or transmitted in any form or by any means, electronic, mechanical, photocopying, or recording, without prior written permission of the Author or Publisher.

Published in 2023 by:

GOSHEN PUBLISHERS LLC
P.O. Box 1562
Stephens City, Virginia, USA
www.GoshenPublishers.com

Our books may be purchased in bulk for promotional, educational, or business use. For inquiries please contact the publisher via email: Agents@GoshenPublishers.com.

First Edition 2023

Cover designed by Goshen Publishers LLC

Printed in the United States of America

All Scriptures are quoted from the King James Version of the Bible unless otherwise noted.

*to every person who feels like
something is missing*

Acknowledgements

To my loving husband, Sylvester Rawlings, thank you for being my biggest cheerleader. You continue to push me to be greater. Your encouragement and love mean everything to me. You have learned to pull me from my comfort zone without damaging me and I appreciate it. I pray this book encourages you to follow me and become a published author. There is certainly a book in you!

To my extremely smart and beautiful daughter, Breia Lassiter, you give me hope that there is more in me. You have been encouraging me to write a book for years. I pray that my courage to step out on faith and accomplish this dream will foster the same courage in you to go and conquer your dreams and make them realities. Your potential is limitless, and I look forward to seeing you soar higher than I can even imagine.

To my handsome and intelligent son, Brandon Lassiter, I wish you could see yourself as I see you. You are brave, capable, and wiser than your years. You are realizing your dreams and making me one proud mama! I hope that my courage to write this book will help show you an example of what is inside of you. I can't wait to see you tap into the God given talent that is waiting to be unleashed on this world that lies within you.

While writing A Christian Journey, my husband and I moved from Maryland to North Carolina. I found myself unable to completely focus and stay true to my routine. However, thanks to my amazing publisher, Dr. Shawn Richmond, who help me to press forward and keep writing even when my brain kept saying I needed to see what the changes, comments, and edits looked like, she encouraged me to trust the process. Although my only knowledge of writing is what I have seen in movies, this process didn't seem right in my mind, but Dr. Shawn, with much patience and gentleness, corralled my fears and propelled me forward. I am so very thankful for her ability to see my vision. I don't believe there would be a finished product without her so thank you, Dr. Shawn, for helping me to get my thoughts on paper and out of my head. You are truly amazing!

Because of Dr. Shawn's brilliance, she partnered me with two truly amazing women as accountability partners, Dr. Kimberly Hayes, and Mrs. Kelli Swinney. These ladies checked on me and encouraged me to keep writing. Their writing victories encouraged me to work harder and be more productive. Thank you, Dr. Hayes, for the idea to set an early morning time schedule to write daily. After I adjusted to the early morning alarm clock, it worked perfectly for me!

As we shared our progress, Kelli would always make me feel like I was doing a good job and that we were in this together. Thank you both for seeing me all the way to the finished line.

Last, but certainly not least, to my good friend and sister in Christ, Pastor Jacqueline Jackson, thank you for always encouraging me to keep writing and believing that I have something to say. Your enthusiasm over the book without having read a single page motivated me to move forward in becoming an author. Thank you for always being in my corner while keeping it real and godly. I truly appreciate our friendship.

Chapter 1

I loved my job! It was exactly what I always wanted to do. Maybe if I kept saying it, I would learn to love getting up so early. I have been working nonstop on an idea to save our clients both money and time. I was so close to figuring it out. I even think about it in my sleep, so I wake up feeling like I just went to bed. I can't afford to be tired today, though, there is an early meeting with the director of the IT department to discuss my design to help companies streamline their businesses.

Only three months after graduating from Texas A&M with a bachelor's degree in Information Technology, it's hard to believe that I'm in Dallas working as an IT Specialist at L&G Technologies, a sought-after company leading the world in global technology. My family was proud of my accomplishments, and I loved doing what I did. Everything was working out great—all but the early mornings. I guessed that was something I would get used to.

Dressed in a navy-blue pinstripe suit with a white button-down blouse and blue stiletto peep-toe heels, I got into my new, sleek black Audi Q5 SUV with the chrome package. I drove the thirty minutes to my office building on Commerce Street, then walked into the building with marble flooring and beautiful plants and seating sprinkled around the reception desk. There were several people already here waiting to be seen. Walking past the security guard's desk, I said good morning. Heading to the elevators, the receptionist said, "Good morning, Chloe! How are you doing?"

I answered, "Good morning. I am doing amazing, but I must hurry upstairs before I am late. Have a great day!"

I head up to the 21st floor, step off the elevator, and walk into my office. L&G Technologies has the entire floor. The offices are extra-large and spacious. The walls are muted gray with colorful paintings covering the walls. Marble floors continue throughout the space with two reception areas and comfortable dark gray couches and chairs for clients and guests to wait.

As soon as I got off the elevator, I was greeted by our amazing office manager and the secretary to the Director of IT, Susan. She runs our office like a well-oiled machine. She is on top of everything that goes on around here, but she is always highly professional and no-nonsense. "Good morning, Susan," I said, excited about my meeting.

Susan replied, "Good morning, Chloe! You look like you are ready to take on the world! Mr. Thomas is in his office. See you in thirty minutes."

I went into my office, which is also a muted gray with a large mahogany desk, matching bookcases, and two very comfortable black swivel chairs for guests. I sat down at my desk and pulled out my notes for the meeting to review. Marcus and Selene, two friends who started here around the same time as I did, came into my office to catch up on weekend news. Selene, dressed in a power red suit with a black blouse and black red-bottom stiletto heels, said, "Good morning, Chloe. How are you doing?"

"I am doing great! Very excited about my meeting with Mr. Thomas this morning. How are you doing?"

Selene said, "I am also great! My weekend was amazing! I met this great guy named Todd at the Cyclone.

We talked and danced for hours. I hope he calls me. I really enjoyed getting to know him."

Marcus, dressed in a gray Armani suit with a white shirt and black and gray tie, is very stylish and handsome. I greeted him. "Hey Marcus! How are you? Did you have a good weekend?"

"I did. I went to a men's conference on Saturday, and the church service on Sunday was exactly what I needed to hear. My pastor seems to always know what is going on with me even though I haven't talked to him. You all really should come visit my church. It will change your life!"

"Oh Marcus, you say that every week. How do you know it will change our lives? How do you know we even want our lives to change?"

"Well, I am just saying, I get something to help me every week. It is like God is speaking directly to me! So, I figure everyone could benefit from having an experience with God like that," he said.

Selene said, "When I go to church, nothing like that ever happens to me. I don't know if I believe you. Plus, Sunday is the day that I sleep in and do my cleaning and laundry."

I chimed in, "I have to agree with Selene. When I go to church, I never feel like God is talking to me, either. So, I am not sure if it works like that, Marcus."

He was quick with his reply. "Maybe you just aren't going to the right church. Maybe you all should come to my church one Sunday."

I was polite but noncommittal. "Maybe we will one Sunday."

Marcus changed the subject. "I hope you have a great meeting with Mr. Thomas. Make sure you come see me afterwards. I want to hear all about it."

I nod. "I will, but right now I need to go over my notes before the meeting. Have a great day, you two!" I shifted my focus to my laptop.

After reading my notes, I felt confident and ready to meet with Mr. Thomas. I went down the hall to his office and saw Susan.

"Is he ready to see me now?"

"Yes," Susan said, "go right in."

I headed into Mr. Thomas's office, which looked like it was three times bigger than mine with couches, chairs, and even a small conference table with four chairs. It has several bookcases full of books and decorations. I greeted him warmly. "Good morning, Mr. Thomas. How are you today?"

"Morning, Chloe! I am well. Please have a seat."

"Thank you, Sir!"

"Chloe, I have been reviewing your project and I am very impressed with the information on how we can help our clients streamline their businesses. Your algorithms seem right on target. I think we should take your idea to the next level and field test it, and I believe you are the right person to head up the operation. I know it has only been three months since you started working here, but you have already proven to be an asset to our company, and I would like to give you this opportunity to test your theory. I am very excited about the possibilities."

"Thank you, Sir! I truly appreciate this opportunity and I believe this will work."

"If it does, I see a promotion very soon in your future. I would like you to meet with Dr. Simmons. He is an IT expert in research and development. He will help you develop the plan and a prototype to see if it works. I have already spoken to him. So, give him a call and set up a meeting. I look forward to hearing how it goes."

"Thank you again, Sir. I appreciate it and I hope you enjoy the rest of your day."

I went back to my office feeling very excited about my meeting with Mr. Thomas. I was not expecting to be selected to head the team to test my theory. It felt a little scary. No, I was not going to think like that. He chose me, so I must be qualified to see it through. I must be confident in my abilities or no one else will be.

I stopped by Marcus' office, which is very similar to mine in size and furniture, to share my good news. "Marcus, you are looking at the new team lead on my project. Can you believe it? I feel like it is a dream!"

"Congratulations, Chloe! You deserve it. You have been working really hard on that project. You can do this!"

"Thank you! I appreciate your confidence in me. I hope this works. I meet with Dr. Simmons next to discuss the way ahead. Wish me luck!"

"Chloe, you don't need luck. You have been blessed by God with this gift. Using it here at work is great, but you must also use it to further His Kingdom."

I was puzzled, "What do you mean Marcus? Why would God be interested in my IT skills? How can my skills help him?"

Evidently, Marcus had been thinking about this. "The church is always in need of web designs and ways to communicate virtually. Those are your skills, and you can help make that happen. Just think about it."

I was not opposed to the idea. "Okay. I will."

"Would you like to celebrate after work? We could meet for dinner and drinks at Malone's."

"Sure, that sounds great. See you later."

"Okay; if you see Selene before I do, please invite her as well. I've got to run. Lots of work to still be done!"

"Okay, we will talk later."

After working for a few hours, Selene stopped by my office. "Hey Chloe! Do you have lunch plans?"

"Hey Selene, I cannot make lunch today. I have calls to make. Did you hear my good news? I am going to be the team lead for my streamline project. Marcus and I are going to dinner after work to celebrate. Do you want to join?"

"Yes, I heard about your good news. Congratulations! Marcus told me. I will see you at Malone's after work."

The rest of the day went by quickly, between meetings and phone calls. I left work and met Marcus and Selene at Malone's for dinner. Malone's was a very nice upscale steakhouse. It had a very large bar area with beautiful dark wood tables and chairs scattered around an enormous wood and brass bar with three brass chandeliers hanging from the ceiling and glass shelves housing every kind of alcohol imaginable.

Marcus said, "The first round is on me! Congratulations again, Chloe! I am super proud of you. Have you spoken with Dr. Simmons?"

"I left a voicemail earlier. I haven't heard back yet. Hopefully, we connect tomorrow."

Selene said, "Rumor has it that Dr. Simmons is not easy to work with. He is brilliant in IT research, but his communication skills are lacking."

I had not heard that about him, but since we would have to work together to get the project off the ground and working, I'd stay optimistic.

After Malone's, I headed home for the night. Walking into my apartment building, I was still amazed that I lived here. The large windows let light shine through brilliantly. Even at night, with the bright stars and streetlights, it is quite inviting. The lobby had chairs and tables scattered around for visitors and the ceilings were twenty feet high with beautiful chandeliers and candle lights to wash the entire space with brightness. The wood-tone accents and pictures provided added warmth and made the space extremely inviting. Having an attendant on duty twenty-four hours a day was a very special touch. It provided safety and ensured all our packages were secured when delivered.

"Good evening, how are you?"

"I am doing great! How are you, Chloe?"

"I am great also. It has been a long day; I am very happy to finally be home."

"Well, don't let me hold you up. Have a good night."

After traveling up to the 15th floor, I was finally in my spacious two-bedroom apartment with eggshell white walls and maple, wide plank wood floors. With my mom's help, I decorated with soft earth tone colors, beige, and olive greens. The curtains were flowing in beige and olive, and the couch was comfortable, with matching pillows and a plush rug on the floor. With an electric chrome fireplace attached to the wall with a television above it, I was totally in love with my first apartment.

Once alone, I started to think about my day and how amazing it turned out. Then I thought about what Marcus said about me being blessed with a gift from God. I never really thought about it like that. *Did God really give this gift to understand technology as a way to help others? Was God really orchestrating all of this? How can I find out the answers to these questions? I have so many questions.... I really need to get to sleep so I can be ready for my new assignment tomorrow.*

I looked down at my phone to see a missed call from Josh. I called him back. "Hi Josh! How are you?"

"Hi Chloe! I am doing great! I was thinking about you and calling to see if you wanted to go out this weekend. I hear there is a new restaurant opening called the Deep Sea. Do you want to check it out?"

"Sure, that sounds like fun. I love seafood and I would love to check out a new restaurant."

"Great! I will make reservations for Saturday night. I will text you the details."

"Sounds good. I look forward to it."

"Well, I have to run. I will talk to you soon."

After a few more calls and scrolling through social media, I went through my routine of getting ready for work the next day, my nightly beauty regime, then got into bed. The thought of my skills being a gift from God came flooding back. I started to wonder if God was like some puppet master, pulling everyone's strings and directing them to His planned outcome. *Was Marcus right? Was I blessed with these gifts from God?* I decided I would go to church on Sunday and see if I could get some answers from God.

The next morning, after arriving at work, I was outlining the process of using my system to streamline businesses when my phone rang.

"Hello, this is Chloe. How may I help you?"

"Good morning, Chloe. This is Dr. Simmons. I received your message, and I am very excited about this new project."

"Good morning, Dr. Simmons. Thank you for returning my call. I am also very excited about this project. Do you have some time to meet with me this morning?"

"I can't meet with you this morning. I have meetings scheduled until lunch time. How about right after lunch? Does one o'clock work for you?"

"Absolutely, would you like to come to my office or yours?"

Dr. Simmons said, "How about I come to your office, since you are the team lead after all."

"Perfect, I will see you at one o'clock."

After a few phone calls and a sandwich at my desk, it was almost one o'clock. I started to get excited about the possibilities of what this project could mean for many businesses and what it could do for my career. Promptly at one, Dr. Simmons arrived. He knocked on my door and came in. He was dressed in a well-tailored navy-blue suit, a light blue shirt, and a navy-blue tie with light blue and orange stripes. He looked very stylish for an older gentleman.

With a smile on his face, he said, "Good afternoon, Chloe, I am Dr. Simmons."

"Good afternoon, Dr. Simmons. Please come in and have a seat. Can I get you something to drink? I have water and juice available."

"No, thank you Chloe. I am not thirsty."

"So, have you had an opportunity to read over my proposal? I really believe this could work."

"Yes, Chloe, I have read it over and it looks very promising; however, I do have a few questions."

Marcus came by later that afternoon. "Hey, Chloe, how is your day going?"

"Hey Marcus, how's it going? I have had a very good day. How was yours?"

"I guess I would say it has been productive. I haven't had a chance to get out of the office all day. Did you hear back from Dr. Simmons?"

"Yes, I did. We met earlier this afternoon. It was a very productive meeting. We set some goals with timelines to get started. He was very focused and seemed excited to be working on this project. He was nothing like Selene described him."

"That's great," Marcus said, "aren't you glad you reserved your judgement until you met with him? Well, I have a conference call in a few minutes. Enjoy the rest of your day."

"You too, Marcus!"

The rest of the day went by quickly and I headed home.

While cooking, my mom called. "Hi Chloe! How are you? I haven't heard from you this week. Is everything ok?"

"Hi Mom! Yes, everything is ok. I have been very busy this week with a new project I am working on. Things are going to be busy over the next few weeks as I get a handle on it."

"That's great, sweetie! I am so very proud of you. I wanted to invite you to dinner on Sunday. Your dad and I want to hear all about this new project."

"Ok Mom, I can do that. I will be over right after church on Sunday."

"Church? You are going to church on Sunday?"

"Yes, I have been thinking about it and I think I need to go."

"Oh, ok. Well, I guess we definitely need to talk. I feel like there is something going on. Are you sure everything is ok?"

"Yes, Mom, I am fine. I will see you at church and then at the house for dinner."

"Perfect! See you on Sunday. I love you, sweetie!"

"I love you too, Mom! Bye!"

After a few more busy workdays, the weekend was finally here! Marcus walked into my office on Friday afternoon. "Hey Chloe!"

"Hey Marcus! What's up? Are you ready for the weekend?"

"Yes," replied Marcus. "I have had an extremely busy week."

"Me too! I am so ready to get out of here and start the weekend. Do you have any plans? Oh no, Marcus, let me guess? You are going to church tonight, right? Of course, you are."

"Well, as a matter of fact, yes, I am going to church tonight. We are having a singles Bible study. Do you want to go?"

"No, not tonight. I have a hair appointment this evening. I have a date tomorrow night with Josh. He is taking me to a restaurant that just recently opened, so I thought I would look my best."

"Well, enjoy your weekend. I will see you on Monday."

"You too, Marcus! See you Monday."

After work and a little pampering, I got home and watched a movie while working on my project, then it was off to bed. I woke up early on Saturday, did a few household chores, then went to the grocery store and stocked up for the week. Next was the nail salon, and then home to prepare for my date with Josh. After trying on several outfits, I settled on a pink and white dress with white sandals to show off my pretty pink toenails. With makeup artistically in place, I looked up as the doorbell rang.

"Hello Josh! Please, come in. I am just about ready." I grabbed my jacket and purse and we headed to the restaurant. The Deep Sea was appropriately named. The restaurant was made to look like you were in the bottom of a boat looking out into the ocean. With several amazing fish tanks, it was very well decorated. The atmosphere was definitely on point.

"Wow, Josh! This place looks awesome! I hope the food is as good as the décor."

After being seated, I said, "Everything on the menu looks good. What are you getting?"

Josh answered, "I think I will have the seafood platter."

"Um, that sounds like a good choice! I think I am going to get the all-you-can-eat shrimp."

After giving the waitress our selections, we chatted about jobs and lives and got caught up on what had been going on. Josh was a commercial litigation attorney with Fisher & Brown, a very prominent law firm in Dallas, Texas.

Josh said, "I was in the courtroom last week and the opposing counsel had botched his case so badly that he approached the judge and asked to be removed from the case. It was totally unbelievable!"

I enjoyed listening to his stories. We were well matched and had common interests. We were both very career driven and not looking for anything serious with relationships, so we work well for each other.

"Any plans for tomorrow?" I asked. "I plan to go to church and then dinner at my parents' house."

"I am meeting my parents at church tomorrow too," exclaimed Josh.

"You know, I have a co-worker, Marcus, who said that every time he goes to church, he feels like God is speaking directly to him, giving him answers to decisions he is considering. I have never had an experience like that, but I sure could use one."

Josh looks puzzled. "What do you mean by that?"

"Well, whenever I am alone, I have this overwhelming feeling that something is missing in me. It is hard to explain, so I hope that when I go to church tomorrow that I will have that experience where God is talking to me and answering my questions like my friend, Marcus."

"Wow, Chloe, that is pretty deep. I have never expe-rienced anything like that before either, so I am interested to know how that turns out."

"Well, I am excited and also a little scared. I mean, I believe in God just like the next person, but I can't even wrap my mind around Him talking to me. I guess we will see tomorrow."

After dinner, Josh took me home, kissed me goodnight, and left. Not much later, I went to bed.

I woke up excited, anticipating that God was going to speak to me and help me to understand this emptiness that I was feeling. I showered, dressed, and headed off to church. Once there, I was greeted by many people who I have not seen in quite a while and, of course, they made me know it, as if I wasn't aware.

One of the church mothers came toward me. They are always so condescending, like they have been saved all their lives. They make me feel like I am unclean or unworthy of even being there. "Blessings, Chloe!"

"Good morning, how are you?"

"I am blessed and highly favored! How have you been?"

"I am well, very busy with work, but very well, thank you."

"Well, you know nothing should come before the Lord, Chloe."

"Yes, ma'am! Nice to see you."

I spoke to my parents and my sister, Crystal, then finally made it to a seat. I wanted to be able to give the pastor my full attention because I was seeking to hear God today.

After the time dedicated to praise and worship, which was always inspiring and uplifting, I was so ready to hear what God had to say to me. I was sure that I was going to get something to help me understand what Marcus was talking about and why I felt so empty.

The pastor took his formal position at the podium and began his sermon. The scripture reference was Luke 15:11–32. He spoke boldly and intently about the prodigal son being in the world, doing everything he was big and bad enough to do, and then having to shamefully come home with nothing to show for it.

He goes on with how loving the father was, how happy he was that his son had come home, and that he didn't even mention anything about all the money he had wasted or what he had been doing while he was away. The pastor drew the correlation between the prodigal son's father and God, our Father, how he waits patiently for us to return to him, and how God forgives us for our wrongdoing, just like the prodigal son's father had. It was a great message, but I didn't feel like God was speaking to me.

I left just as empty as I felt when I had arrived. I was disappointed because I really was expecting to hear something that would explain what was going on with me. *What was this emptiness that kept trying to consume me?* I wasn't sure how to get my answers now that this had not worked.

CHAPTER 2

Everyone was just getting back from church and starting to get dinner going when I walked in at my parents' house. I went to my dad and hugged him.

"Hey Dad!" My dad was a tall man with salt and pepper hair, glasses, and a dazzling smile. He always seemed to be happy, as if his life was the best.

"Hey Chloe," he said. "How are you?"

"I am great! How are you doing, Dad?"

"Oh, I am loving life. I am getting ready to enjoy some football. You want to join me?"

"Maybe later. I am going to see if Mom needs help in the kitchen."

As I walked into the kitchen, I heard my mom saying to my sister, "Is that Chloe I hear?"

"Yes, Mom, it's me. What's going on in here?" My mom had cooked like there were going to be one hundred people. "Why so much food? Are you expecting other guests? It's just the four of us, right?"

My mom, who was always planning and preparing something, said, "Of course it is just the four of us. I wanted to make sure there was enough, and you and your sister can take leftovers home for lunch tomorrow."

Well, who can argue with that? What a great idea. My mom, forever the entertainer, always had a luncheon, dinner, gathering, or something else she was preparing for.

My sister, Crystal, was a registered nurse at Dallas Memorial Hospital. It's not just a job for her, it truly is a calling. She loves to help people. Together, we set the table beautifully, just like Mom taught us when we were little, and called my dad to come and eat.

After we all sat and filled our plates, my mom started with the questions. "So, Chloe, how is the project coming?"

"I met with the R&D specialist, and he thinks my idea is possible, so we are building the system now so we can test it. I am very hopeful that it will help companies streamline their business processes."

Mom started, "Not that I wasn't pleased to see you in church today, but what made you want to come?"

"Well, I am not sure if I can clearly explain it, but I have been feeling like something is missing in my life and nothing and no one has been able to fill that void. A friend that I work with, who goes to church all the time, keeps telling me how amazing God is in his life and how he can tell that it is God orchestrating it all. I must admit that I don't really understand what he is talking about, so I thought maybe I needed to come to church to see if God would speak to me and help me figure out this emptiness that continues to haunt me."

"Well, did it work? Did God speak to you today?" my sister asked.

"Unfortunately, I didn't get the answers I was seeking. So, I am not sure what to do now."

My mom said, "You know, listening to the message today, I got the sense that it was for you. I mean, I know you are not the prodigal daughter that we sent off with your inheritance and you came back empty-handed, but maybe being away from church for a period and coming back because you are empty and looking for something is kind of the same concept."

"Well, the church mother certainly didn't show me that unconditional love that the father showed his son, so I am not sure if this is the same."

"We were indeed happy to see you."

"Of course, you were, but you would have been happy to see me no matter where you saw me. I know this may sound crazy, but something is missing, and I can't even explain what it is I am looking for. I can't explain it and I don't even know how or where to get the answers to the questions that I can't explain. I just need to know where do I go from here."

"Chloe, I believe if you ask God, He will answer you. You should try there. Pray to God and ask Him to help you. Our pastor says when we don't even know what to say, God knows, and He will respond. Give that a try and see how He responds."

"Thanks, Mom, I will."

Dinner was delicious and it was really nice spending the evening with my family. I helped my sister wash the dishes and clean Mom's kitchen before heading home for the night.

Once I got home, I checked my schedule for tomorrow to see what my day was going to look like, answered a few emails, and made a few notes to handle tomorrow, then closed my computer. After getting ready for bed, I decided to get on my knees and pray.

"Dear God, it's me, Chloe. Thank you for your word today on the prodigal son. I am not sure if that was for me, but I wanted to know why I feel this emptiness inside. I have a very full life, I have an amazing career that I love, a family who loves me and who I love, I have great friends and an active social schedule. I am very happy with my life, so why do I have this feeling that something is missing? I have chosen not to have a serious romantic relationship and I am happy with that choice, so I don't think that is what's missing, but I am clear that something is missing. Can you help me identify what is missing and help me to find it? Thank you, God! Amen."

I got into bed and went to sleep. For the first time in months, I fell asleep without feeling that overwhelming sense of emptiness. When I woke up, I felt refreshed and ready for my day. After showering and having a cup of coffee, I dressed in a gray suit with black pinstripes, a black blouse, and black stilettos. I left for work with minutes to spare and arrived early enough to stop at Starbucks for a cup of coffee and a muffin. I saw Selene at the coffee shop.

"Hi Selene!"

"Hi Chloe!"

"How was your weekend?"

"It was great! I went to the Cyclone on Saturday night with that guy I told you I met last weekend. We danced all night. He is a really fun guy! How was your weekend?"

"My weekend was nice. Josh and I went to dinner at that new restaurant, the Deep Sea. The food was amazing and you really feel like you are at the bottom of a ship. I love your dress!"

Selene was in a yellow dress with purple flowers. It was flowing and gathered at her waist with a purple blazer. She wore deep purple peek-toe sandals to finish her ensemble.

"Thanks Chloe! You always look amazing in your tailored suits. I guess we better get to the office before we are late."

We walked into our building and got on the elevator, chatting away about fashion and food. We got off the elevator and Selene said, "Have a good day, Chloe."

"You too," I said.

"Maybe we can do lunch. Give me a call when you see how your day is going."

"Okay."

"See you later."

I said, "Good morning, Sarah!"

"Good morning, Chloe!"

I continued down the hall to my office. Once inside, I opened my computer and started with the list I made the night before. I had a message from Dr. Simmons saying he wanted to see me when I got in. *That can't be good. I wonder what is going on.*

When I got to Dr. Simmons' office, there were computers and computer screens everywhere. Many of the computers were running nonstop data across the screen. I walked up to Dr. Simmons and said, "Hello, I just received your message. Why did you want to see me? Is everything okay with the program?"

He said, "Hello, Chloe. Thank you for coming to see me so quickly. I wanted to show you how the program was responding to the parameters we set. The sequence is not responding at all as we expected. It appears like this won't work."

"Oh no, I was so sure it would work." I started to pace back and forward as I thought about solutions to this problem. "Can I take a look at the data?" I asked.

I took a seat and began to review the data that was input. "I was so sure this would work. From everything I tried, it seemed extremely positive that this would work."

I continued to pore over the data, checking to make sure there were no errors in the information that was put in. As I checked and double checked, I noticed some inconsistencies in the input information. Something was definitely off. I started from the beginning and input the data again and clicked enter, then information began to scroll across the screen.

The computer was giving me all the information that I needed to streamline the business practices. It worked! I showed the results to Dr. Simmons.

He said, "This is amazing, Chloe. I don't know what we did wrong, but this really does work."

I walked him through what I had done to get the information and we tested the product on another business. It worked again. I was so excited to see the idea becoming a reality.

Dr. Simmons started building trends and comparisons to show Mr. Thomas. I left Dr. Simmons and went back to my office to complete my part of the presentation for Mr. Thomas. This was really happening! I could hardly contain my excitement. I worked for hours building the presentation with slides and supporting data to explain how the program worked and what type of information could be extracted from the program.

Chapter 3

Marcus came to my office and knocked on the door. I looked up. "Hey, Marcus! How are you?"

"Hey, Chloe! I am great!"

"What's up?"

"Not too much, except my program worked! Can you believe it? It really worked! Dr. Simmons and I did a test run today and it worked! I mean, he has to do more tests to confirm, but from what we saw today, it looks like it works! I am so excited."

"Congratulations, Chloe! I am so happy for you. I have to say, I am not surprised. You have a really good eye for coding and properties."

"Oh Marcus, it was so exhilarating to see the preliminary findings. This has been a really good day. Marcus, do you have a few minutes? Can you come in and shut the door?"

"Sure, what's up, Chloe?"

"Well, I was thinking about our discussion last week about God and my gifts and His expectations. Do you remember?"

"Yes, I do," smiled Marcus.

"Well, I went to church on Sunday hoping that He would speak to me about some things I have been feeling and thinking about. Marcus, don't look at me like that! I'm not crazy! I just don't really understand all this God stuff and I wanted to get some clarification."

"Chloe! What do you mean clarification? Do you think God is like your computer? That you can just type a few questions in, and He will spit out the answers to you?" Laughing, he said, "Chloe, that is not exactly how it works!"

"Well, Marcus, exactly how does it work?"

"Chloe, I don't have time to explain it all to you right now. What are you doing after work? Maybe we can meet for dinner, and I can explain what I know. I really suggest you talk to my pastor, but I will do my best to answer your questions."

"Okay, Marcus, that sounds good. I need to get back to work on my presentation, but after work I am all yours. I really want to understand."

"Okay, I will do my best to help you."

After a few more hours of emails, phone calls and meetings, it was finally the end of the day. Marcus came by my office and said, "Are you ready to head out?"

"Yes, I absolutely am! What a busy day! Did it seem like today was like two days in one? I feel like they got two or three days out of me today!"

"Yes, it has been a very busy day for me as well. Let's get out of here!"

"Okay. So, where are we going?"

"I thought we could go to Marcy's Café on 5th Street. They have delicious food, and it is quieter. We should be able to talk and eat comfortably."

"Okay, that sounds good. I do love their food. Let's go, I will meet you there."

We got to Marcy's, went in, and were seated quickly. Marcy's is very old school with waitresses who wear uniform dresses with aprons over them. They still use paper tickets to take your orders. There are booths, tables, and a bar counter with seats. It reminds me of an old fifties diner, but the food is out of this world.

Once we ordered, I said, "So, Marcus, I prayed and asked God why I was feeling empty like this and I didn't really get an answer, so I decided to go to church on Sunday. I really expected to get some answers there. I still have no idea what it is that I am even feeling to explain it to anyone, other than an emptiness. I am not sure how you are going to help me, but I am willing to listen."

Marcus said, "Although I am not really sure what you are feeling, maybe if I explain to you how I came to know Christ that may help you. Two years ago, I was invited by my friend to his church. He said they had a single's ministry, and they were always getting together fellowshipping. So, my first thought was that there would be single ladies there and that sounded good to me. I asked him what kind of things they did, and he said gospel concerts, bowling, skating, Bible study, etc. So, I said, let me know the next time you all meet.

"A few weeks later, he called and said they were having a Bible study and then going out to eat afterwards on Friday and asked if I wanted to go. I was free, so I said, sure, send me the information. On Friday, I thought about canceling, but something stopped me. Like, I got so busy at work that before I knew it, it was time to go and I had not called and canceled. So, I went, and there were about thirty people there, all close to my age.

"We sat in a classroom and the youth pastor, Pastor J, who looked like he was maybe thirty years old, stood up and he greeted us and welcomed us to the Bible study and then he said we were going to be talking about integrity that night. He talked about doing what is right even when no one is looking. He read the story of Moses when he killed the Egyptian and hid the body. Pastor J was so cool and relatable when he was sharing the story that he had me practically sitting on the edge of my seat to hear it.

"He was transparent and shared his own experience and then others opened up and shared. I felt like I was in a group therapy session. Something prompted me to share a story of my own. In my mind I was thinking, what am I doing? Why am I telling these total strangers my business? But it was so freeing, and it felt like such a safe place that I could share openly and freely. I didn't know then what I know now—that the Holy Spirit was prompting me to share."

I said, "Marcus, you are going to have to explain that. How do you know it was the Holy Spirit?"

"You know me, Chloe, do I readily share my private life in group settings? Have you ever known me to open up about my personal stuff with anyone other than you and Selene? See, this was different. Something moved me to open my mouth and speak. It's like it wasn't me talking. I mean, it was me, but it was very uncharacteristic of me. So, I have since learned more about the Holy Spirit and what He does. How He is able to prick our hearts in whatever direction He needs us to follow.

"For example, have you ever wanted to go to a place and you were so excited about going? In your mind, you really wanted to be there because it was going to be so much fun, but then something else inside of you was telling you not to go. It is like a war going on inside of you on whether you should go. This only happens to saved people. Those who have the Holy Spirit on the inside of them will find they have this conflict happening within them."

"As strange as this sounds, Marcus, I can relate to being conflicted sometimes about my decisions, so I think I understand what you are saying."

"I know it may sound strange; imagine how I felt as I started to share things that I have never told anyone, especially in a group setting. After the Bible study ended, I got a chance to speak to Pastor J and I told him how strange it felt to share the personal details that I shared but how compelled I felt to share. He said, 'Aww man, that was just the Holy Spirit working on you'.

"I was like, what are you talking about? He said, 'Here is my card, give me a call and I will be happy to explain it to you'. Afterwards, we all went to Applebee's for dinner and enjoyed more fellowship with light and funny conversations. I really enjoyed meeting everyone and I connected with a few of them on social media and began hanging out with them and getting to know them.

"They didn't just go to church on Sunday and Bible study on Wednesday nights, they had study groups all during the week and prayer calls. I asked my friend, why do you all have to study the Bible every day? He said, 'We don't have to, we choose to'. He said it was like starting a relationship with someone. The only way to get to know them more closely is to spend more time with them.

"So, the only way to really know God is to study and read His word daily for yourself. That is how we get the knowledge and wisdom that God has for us. We can't get that in the fullness if we are only listening to someone preach once a week for about thirty minutes. With that understanding, I dove in and began my own reading and studying of God's word and I have never looked back."

"Wow, Marcus, that is amazing. I love the analogy of getting to know God like we get to know each other. That makes perfect sense to me. I think I would like to go to that Bible study."

"That is great news! We are actually having class this Friday at 7pm. You should come with me."

"I will. Thank you so much for sharing with me. I hope God will help me with this emptiness that keeps haunting me."

When we finished eating, it was getting late. I left Marcus, went home, and got ready for bed with so many thoughts about what Marcus had shared. This Holy Spirit must be something powerful to get him to open up in front of so many strangers and share his story. Maybe He knows what we need more than we do? I was looking forward to going to the Bible study on Friday.

Chapter 4

I woke up refreshed and ready for the day. Dressing in a caramel skirt suit with a beige blouse and brown heels, I switched out my purse while my coffee was brewing. I put my coffee in a to-go cup, grabbed my computer and purse, and headed out the door.

Arriving at work, I immediately got to work polishing my proposal, including Dr. Simmons' analysis, which he had emailed me. It was really starting to take shape. I sent my draft to Dr. Simmons for his input and then turned my attention to some other projects that needed my input. Afterward, I answered emails and returned a few calls before I headed to the coffee shop for a quick lunch. There I ran into Selene.

"Hey, Selene! How are you doing?"

"I am doing good. It has been a very busy morning, but I am happy for a little break."

"Do you want to share a table for lunch or do you have to get back?" I asked.

She said, "Sure."

We got our lunches and, of course, coffee and headed for a table to catch up. I said, "So, what's new with you?"

"I have been hanging out with the guy I met at Cyclone. He is so much fun and we enjoy some of the same things. Last night we went to the Mirage and danced the night away. You know how much I enjoy dancing and so does he. We had a great time. Of course, I am exhausted today, but it was totally worth it."

"Sounds like fun, you do love to dance. How is work going?"

"Well," Selene started, "I am struggling on this new project. I am not sure what Mr. Thomas is looking for. He has sent it back to me three times. Maybe he just doesn't like me."

"Come on, Selene, that's not fair. I don't think Mr. Thomas is like that. Maybe you should see if you can get on his calendar and have a meeting to see if you can get some clarification on the project."

"Just because he made you a team lead, all of a sudden you like him? Please, I heard he doesn't even think your project is going to work."

"Really? Who told you that?"

"I just heard it. How are you doing with Dr. Simmons? I told you he was hard to work with."

"So far, Dr. Simmons has been easy to work with. He has been attentive to the project and has met every deadline. I have not had any problems working with him. You might want to check your sources."

"Everything seems to go smoothly for you, Chloe! Oh well, I better get back to work. I don't want to have to stay late. I have a dinner date tonight."

"You are going out with Cyclone dude again tonight?"

"No, I have a dinner date with someone else."

"Oh, I thought you said you really like Cyclone dude."

"I do, but I like Mike, Tony, and Ron too."

"Ah, I see! Well, enjoy the rest of your day and your dinner tonight."

After Selene left, I laughed to myself. That girl was too much. I left the coffee shop and headed back to work. When I got to my office, I got a text from Selene saying, *I meant to ask you, did you hear that Josh was dating Janet?*

I responded, *My Josh?*

Yes girl, they were seen at that restaurant he took you to the other night.

Really? No, I had not heard that. Plus, Josh and I are just friends who occasionally go out. He can date whomever he chooses.

I thought you might want to know since you were dating him.

Well, thanks for letting me know, but again it's cool. I put my cell phone away thinking, wow, that girl is messy. Is she trying to cause trouble? I don't have time for this. I have work to do.

I got back to work. There was an email from Dr. Simmons with a few tweaks on my proposal that I incorporated. I felt ready to send the proposal to Mr. Thomas and was really pleased with how it turned out. Quickly typing, I emailed Dr. Simmons back and said, I am sending it to Mr. Thomas, cross your fingers! After pushing the send button, I shut my computer off and prepared to go home for the day.

Leaving my office, I ran into Selene again. She was standing around a few co-workers talking about me and Josh. When she noticed me, she said, "You are leaving early, is everything okay?"

It hurt me to hear Selene talking about me. I thought we were friends, but I refuse to stoop to her pettiness, so I pretended I hadn't heard her conversation about me. "Everything is great," I said. "I just sent my proposal to Mr. Thomas, and I believe he is going to be happy with it."

"Can you look at my project? I could really use another set of eyes on it. I told you Mr. Thomas has sent it back three times already."

"Sure, send it to me and I will look at it tonight."

"Thanks, Chloe, I appreciate it. Hey, Chloe, you aren't mad at me for telling you about Josh, are you?"

"Why would I be mad? Josh is free to date whom he pleases."

"Okay, I just didn't want you to be mad at me."

"I will see you tomorrow, Selene. Have a good night."

"You too, Chloe! Good night."

I got in my car and drove off, wondering what was going on with Selene. She talked like she was happy with her life, but she seemed very unhappy. She used to have this sparkle in her eyes when she would talk about projects and deadlines. Now all she seemed to talk about was hanging out and dancing the night away with the flavor of the week. It's as if she needed to have something to tell people that she thought would make them envy her, and that sparkle is definitely gone. I would talk to her tomorrow about what I overheard.

This evening, there was little traffic and I got home quickly. Afterward, I put a few chicken breasts into the oven and steamed some broccoli. After dinner, I opened my computer and began to look at Selene's project. It was poorly written and didn't make sense. It seemed like she rushed to put something together just to say she had completed the assignment. That was very unusual for Selene.

Usually, her thoughts were focused and concise. I decided to print the document out and put my changes in the margins so that no one else would be privy to my help except her.

It took a while. There were changes on almost every page of the seventy-page document. What in the world was going on? This didn't even look like Selene's work. I put the document in my work bag and checked a few emails before signing off for the night.

Josh called.

"Hello Josh! How are you?"

"I am good. How are you, Chloe?"

"I am great!"

"How is that project going?"

"It is going even better than I expected. I emailed my boss the completed proposal earlier today."

"That's wonderful! I am glad it is going so well."

"What's new with you?"

"Not much, just busy as usual."

"Do you have any plans this weekend? Do you want to hang out?"

"Yes, I do have plans this weekend. Maybe we can get together another time?"

"No problem, that's cool. I do have some good news I wanted to share. I was offered a new job at one of our other law offices in San Diego. I have been considering taking the job. It is a pay increase, but also a much heavier workload. I am not sure about leaving Dallas, but I am weighing my options."

"That is wonderful news, Josh! I am very happy for you. Is there anything or anyone special keeping you here in Dallas? I know your family is here and some close friends, so I am sure you will always come back to visit, but is there someone you might not want to leave?"

"Well, now that you mention it, Janet and I have been spending a lot of time together. I probably should not be talking to you about this, but we are friends, right?"

"Of course, we are friends, and you can talk to me about anything."

"So, Janet and I have gotten pretty close over the past few months. I don't know if I would say that I could not live without her, but I am not sure if I want to leave her either."

"Not that you asked my opinion, but I think you should talk this over with Janet and see what she says. Maybe together you can figure out a way to make everything work out. If she is important enough to you for you to pause before accepting the job, then this is a decision you should at least discuss together. Either way, I am glad that we can talk about these things because your friendship means a lot to me. I will miss you if you leave, but it will give me somewhere to visit. Well, I guess I should get ready for my day tomorrow. I am expecting to hear from Mr. Thomas about my project. Let me know when you decide about the move. I will talk to you soon."

"Okay! Sounds good. Have a good night, Chloe. You helped me more than you know. Goodbye!"

I hung up feeling good, knowing that my friendship with Josh was as strong as ever. I felt happy for him and Janet. I hoped they were able to have it all. Tired, I got ready for bed, then slept soundly, not even feeling the normal emptiness that I usually felt.

The next morning, I woke up feeling energized after a good night's sleep. After a cup of coffee, showering and dressing in a blush pink and beige dress with a beige blazer and matching heels, I left for work. When I got to my office door, I saw Selene headed my way.

"Good morning, Chloe!"

"Good morning, Selene! When you get a chance, can you come and see me?"

"Sure Chloe, I will be there right after I put my things in my office."

I went inside my office and turned on my computer and began reading emails and making a list of phone calls I needed to make. There was an email from Mr. Thomas congratulating me on a job well done on my project. He wanted to meet with me and Dr. Simmons on what was next, so I made a note to get on Mr. Thomas' schedule as soon as possible.

Just then, Selene knocked on my door. She asked, "Chloe, can I come in?"

"Yes, Selene, please come in." After Selene got settled into her seat, I pulled out the printed document and handed it to her. I said, "I thought I would print the document and make the changes so that my changes would not be visible to everyone reviewing the document. I hope this helps you."

"Thank you, Chloe! I appreciate you reviewing my document."

"I was confused by some of the mistakes. They were very basic and should have been caught. It made me wonder if you are getting bored with your job or if something else may be going on with you. I mean, your work used to be meticulous without even a typo, but this document didn't even seem like you wrote it."

"I don't know what you mean. Are you trying to imply that I am passing off someone else's work?"

"No, I wasn't implying anything, but we have reviewed each other's work many times in the past, and this document just seems very different from your past work. I am only bringing this up because if I can see it, then more than likely so can Mr. Thomas. I am just trying to help you like you asked. Anyway, I have a meeting in a few minutes, so I hope my changes help you. I will talk to you later."

I couldn't believe how sensitive Selene got about her document. She'd asked me to read it. I was just giving her my feedback. Oh well, enough about her, I told myself. I have my own project to think about. I called Sarah to get a few time slots for my meeting with Mr. Thomas and Dr. Simmons, then called Dr. Simmons to see which time worked best for him. Then I called Sarah back and scheduled our meeting for tomorrow at 2pm.

After several phone calls, project revisions, and way too many emails, it was time to head home. I was packing up my things when Selene came to my office.

She said, "I wanted to thank you for reviewing my project. After making your suggested changes, I sent it to Mr. Thomas and he finally gave me the green light to move forward."

"You are welcome, Selene. I still don't understand what is going on with you, but I am glad you can move forward on your project."

"I am good, Chloe. I just needed some help, so thank you. Are you leaving now?"

"Yes, I am. How about you?"

"No, I have one more email I need to get out before I call it a night."

"Okay, well enjoy your evening. See you tomorrow."

"Good night, Chloe!"

When I got home, my mom called. She said, "Hey, Chloe! How are you?"

"I am fine, Mom. How are you?"

"I am doing great! I was just wondering if I would see you at church on Sunday."

"I don't know, I may have to work. I have a meeting with Mr. Thomas tomorrow about my project on the way ahead, so I am not sure what my weekend is going to entail."

"How have you been? Are you still feeling like something is missing?"

"Although it hasn't been affecting my sleep as much, I still have the same nagging feeling."

"I was talking to the pastor about it the other day, and he said it sounds like Jesus is calling you."

"What do you mean? Calling me for what?"

"You do know that Jesus chooses us and calls us to salvation. I mean, we hear people say, I gave my life to Christ today, but they should be saying Christ chose me today. That's what Pastor was teaching on this week in Bible study. It was a great lesson. Anyway, I was thinking you should meet with Pastor and talk to him about how you are feeling."

"I was talking to Marcus the other day and he said something along the same lines to me. His church has a singles ministry that I was planning to check out. I think they meet next week."

"I like the sounds of a singles ministry for you. You might meet a husband."

"Okay, Mom, I guess it is time to end this conversation."

"Oh Sweetie, I am just kidding, sort of. I am proud of you for staying focused on your career. Now, you might want to think about your personal life. Just give it some thought."

"I have to check on my dinner."

"Let me know about church. I will talk to you later. I love you!"

"I love you too, Mom. Bye."

Next, I opened my computer and checked my emails, answered a few and then made a list of things to do tomorrow to prepare for my meeting with Mr. Thomas. I checked the weather, picked out something to wear for tomorrow, and got ready for bed. Once in bed, my mind went back to Selene and how offended she got about her document. I sent up a prayer for her and then quickly fell asleep.

I woke up early and well rested. Maybe I was finally adjusting to this early morning living. I got up and dressed in an olive pants suit with a beige button-down shirt, and paired my ensemble with olive pumps and a matching laptop bag. I made a cup of coffee to go and went off to work.

Once in the building, I walked into my office, confident and ready to begin my day. In the hallway, I ran into Marcus.

"Hi Marcus, how are you doing?"

"Hey Chloe, I am doing wonderful. What's new with you?"

"Not much, just preparing to meet with Mr. Thomas today about the next step in my project."

"That's great! I am very proud of you. I know you know how unusual it is to catch the attention of upper management so early in your career. I have been hearing your name mentioned over and over by the gossip group."

"You know I don't listen to that nonsense. I do my best to steer clear of that group."

"I do too, but I still manage to pick up things from time to time and let me tell you…you are hot news! I even caught something about a run in between you and Selene."

"Oh please, that was nothing. It seemed like she was trying to stir up trouble between me and Josh, but it didn't work. We discussed it like adults, and all is well. I even helped her with her project the other day."

"I am glad to hear that things are nothing like the picture that the gossip group painted. By the way, are you still planning to go to our single's group Bible study tomorrow?"

"Absolutely, I am looking forward to it."

"Great! I better get to work. Hopefully, I will see you later."

"I'll see you later. Have a great day, Marcus!"

I answered a few emails, returned a few calls, and then ran out to pick up lunch. I saw Selene at the café across the street eating lunch. I walked in, greeting her and those at her table, then placed my to-go order and waited for it to get ready. Selene walked over and asked me if I wanted to join them.

"Thanks, but not today. I have something I need to finish as soon as possible. I just stopped long enough to pick something up. I will be working through lunch."

"Oh, okay. Well, enjoy your lunch. Maybe I will see you later this afternoon."

"Sounds good! Enjoy your lunch as well."

She went back to her table and started talking to the others. I felt sure I was being talked about, but I didn't have time to be worried about that. The waitress called my number, I got my lunch, and left to go back to work. As I ate, I wrote down my ideas on what should be done next on my project to see if they would match up with Mr. Thomas' ideas.

Two o'clock finally arrived and I grabbed my pad and pen and headed to Mr. Thomas's office. Dr. Simmons was already there. I walked up to him. "Good afternoon, Dr. Simmons."

"Good afternoon, Chloe! How are you?"

"I am doing wonderful. Thank you for asking. How are you, sir?"

"I am doing great! Are you ready for what's next?"

"I hope so."

Sarah said, "Mr. Thomas will see you now."

We walked into Mr. Thomas's office.

"Good afternoon, Mr. Thomas."

"Good afternoon, Chloe and Dr. Simmons. Please, have a seat and let's get started."

We all sat down and began discussing the project. The meeting went extremely well, and I was right on target as to the way ahead and what was next to be done. Dr. Simmons and I left Mr. Thomas's office with a clear understanding of how to proceed and what was expected.

Mr. Thomas was such a great communicator. He explained his expectations very clearly. Walking down the hall, I said to Dr. Simmons, "Do you have a few minutes to go over some of thoughts that came to mind during the meeting?"

"Sure, let's meet in your office in five minutes."

I said, "Okay. See you there."

I stopped in the ladies room and then met Dr. Simmons in my office. We sat down and began discussing our thoughts. After about thirty minutes, it seemed we had a good game plan for what each of us would do.

He left my office, and I immediately started working on my part. When I looked up at the clock, it was 6pm. I said, "Oh wow, I didn't realize it was so late."

I shut things down and got ready to leave for the day. The offices were dark and quiet. Most people were already gone. I locked up and left too.

When I got home, I got comfortable and started to cook some dinner. I seasoned chicken breasts and put them in the oven, then cut vegetables to make a salad. When the chicken was done, I added it to the salad and dinner was ready. Right after dinner, Selene called.

"Hi Chloe!"

"Hi Selene! How are you?"

"I am exhausted. I had such a long day today. I tried to come and see you several times, but I could not get away."

"I understand, my day was extremely busy too. I looked up and could not believe it was already 6pm."

"I left about 5:30. I didn't know you were still working. I assumed you were gone. Wow. Sounds like we had the same type of day."

"So, what's up?"

"Since tomorrow is Friday, I wanted to see if you wanted to go to McGuire's for happy hour?"

"Sorry, I can't. I already have plans. I promised Marcus I would go to Bible study with him tomorrow."

"Bible study? Who are you and where is my friend Chloe?"

"Real funny. You know he has been asking us forever to go with him, well I decided to go. How about you go with us?"

"No thanks, I plan to celebrate my project tomorrow. It is finally headed in the right direction and those edits helped to get us there, so I just wanted to thank you."

"Oh wow! That is awesome news! I am happy for you."

"Raincheck on the happy hour?"

"Absolutely! So, no date tonight?"

"No, maybe later tomorrow after happy hour."

"Oh okay! What about you? Have you talked to Josh?"

"Yes, I talked to him a few days ago. He is busy as usual and has been offered a job in San Diego."

"San Diego! Wow! That is awesome. I would love to live in California."

"Well, there are a lot of things to consider. His whole life is here, his family, friends, and all things familiar. I may call him tomorrow to see if he has decided."

"I know if he moves, you will miss him."

"I would miss him, but I will be happy for him either way. I told him if he moved, it would give me somewhere new to visit. So, I guess we will see what he decides."

"What did you find out about him and Janet?"

"I told you, Josh and I are just friends. He can be with whomever he chooses. There was nothing to find out."

"Okay! I know you like Josh."

"You also know that we have been nothing but friends who occasionally went out. There was never more than that."

"I always thought you two made the perfect couple. He seemed perfect for you."

"We are perfect as friends."

"Okay, I won't push anymore. I better go, I am headed out to dinner. I will see you tomorrow."

"Okay, goodbye."

I opened my computer to check my emails and plan my day for tomorrow. After answering a few emails and making a list of things to do tomorrow, I closed my computer. My thoughts turned to my conversation with Selene. She seemed more like herself tonight than she had been. I hoped whatever was going on was over now. She didn't share much about herself. She never talks about her family or her past. I would try to meet up with her next week for dinner. I watched TV for a while and then it was off to bed.

The next morning, I walked into the break room and heard some ladies talking about me choosing to go to church tonight versus celebrating Selene. Rolling my eyes, I thought, news travels like lightning in this place. I pretended not to hear what they were talking about and made myself a cup of coffee. I said, "Good morning!" They each said good morning and left the room. I was feeling a little offended. Selene didn't seem upset about me missing her celebration tonight, but maybe she was.

Maybe those ladies just took things out of proportion; they love being messy. This office could certainly be called Peyton Place! There was always someone talking about someone. I left the break room and went to my office and closed my door. I didn't want to hear any more of the office gossip this morning. I got to work, and when my stomach started to growl I knew it must be close to lunch time. Someone knocked on my door, I called out to come in.

"Hi Chloe," Marcus said.

"Hey Marcus! How are you?"

"I am blessed! How are you, Chloe?"

"I am good, excited about going to your singles' Bible study tonight."

"Great! I am glad to know you are still planning to go. I heard that Selene was inviting people to McGuire's this evening for a celebration. I thought you might have decided to go celebrate with Selene."

"It did cross my mind, but as happy as I am that Selene's project is starting to move forward, I am not sure I understand why that is a reason to celebrate. Seems like she is just celebrating doing her job!"

"That is exactly what I thought! I am glad that I am not the only one thinking like that!"

"Are you going to lunch?"

"Yes, I am starving! Do you have time for lunch today?"

"Yes, I was headed to the café across the street."

"Sounds good, let me get my purse and I will go with you."

We got to the café and, of course, Selene and her posse were there.

"Hey, ladies! Enjoying your lunch?"

"Hi Chloe, Hi Marcus! Would you like to join us?"

"Looks like you all are finishing up. Maybe next time."

We got in line, ordered our food and then found a table. After we got our food, we settled in to eat. Marcus prayed over our food and then we started catching up. We could feel eyes on us, but we didn't acknowledge it. We just talked, laughed, and enjoyed each other's company.

A few minutes later, Selene said, "See you all back at the office."

Marcus and I said, "Okay," and went back to our conversation.

Once they left, I said, "You know we are their topic of conversation all the way back to the office."

"I know! What else is new? I am used to them talking about me. Does it bother you?"

"Nope, I don't care. I am used to being the subject of attention. I have been ignoring it all my life."

"Really? I always thought you were more of an in-crowd type girl."

"Absolutely not! I was never in the in-crowd. I was the one walking down the hall alone and hearing whispers as I walked by. The same way I do around our office. That's why I keep my door closed a lot. I don't want to hear the gossip going by. Selene seems to be caught up right in the middle of it all. I think she likes the attention that she gets from appearing to be in the know. Oh well, I pray she starts making some different choices before it affects her job."

"Me too! So, do you want to get something to eat before we head to Bible study?"

"I thought you said you all usually eat afterwards."

"We do, but I usually pick up something light before Bible study too."

"Okay, where and what time do you want to meet?"

"Meet me at Applebee's on W. Illinois Avenue at 5:30pm."

"Sounds good! I will see you there."

I went back to work wondering what God would say to me tonight.

Chapter 5

I met Marcus at Applebee's and we had a light dinner. I left my car parked there and rode with him to the church. We walked in, and Marcus introduced me to several people. There were around forty young adults there. After we settled in, Pastor J, who was the youth pastor, prayed, then several people stood up and gave testimonies that amazed me. I would have just thought that I was lucky that I didn't get hurt when I got into that accident, but the way they explained what happened and how God showed up to protect them gave me a different perspective on things that happen in my life.

After the testimonies, Pastor J stood, opened his Bible, and said, "Tonight, we are going to be talking about seeing an invisible God."

Immediately, I thought, *that doesn't even make sense. How can you see something that is invisible?*

Pastor J was literally saying the same thing out loud. Then he asked us to turn to the book of Colossians, Chapter 1:15–16. He read the scripture which says: *He is the image of the invisible God, the firstborn of all creation. For by him all things were created, in heaven and on earth, visible and invisible, whether thrones or dominions or rulers or authorities—all things were created through him and for him.*

He started out talking about how we may find it difficult to believe in God because we can't see Him physically. He said then, "We can't see air, but I think we can all agree that we believe it exists. Have you ever stopped to think about why you woke up this morning, but others didn't? Have you ever wondered why you are generally healthy and hardly ever get sick, while others are always in poor health? Have you ever heard about a traffic jam on the highway and said I am so glad I woke up late today or that I am working from home today? How about this one…why some of us got COVID and others didn't? Our invisible God is showing up for us in all these instances. He is keeping us safe and directing our paths. It is His breath that He breathed into us that Moses talks about in creation over in Genesis 2:7 where it says: *'then the Lord God formed the man of dust from the ground and breathed into his nostrils the breath of life, and the man became a living creature.'* Every morning we wake up, God has given us a gift of life."

Pastor J went on to give other examples of us being able to see this invisible God. Others were chiming in with questions and thoughts about things happening in their life and saying "thank you, God" because they recognized that it could have only been God who fixed the problem or healed their body.

It was like a lightbulb went off in me. I started to remember situations in my life and how it all worked out, like when I was in college. One day, I was down to my last dollar and I was looking for change to go to the vending machine. The CashApp chime went off and one of my aunts had put some money in my account because she was thinking about me.

Also, growing up, my sister seemed to get sick constantly, but I hardly ever sneezed. We lived in the same house, ate the same food, and had the same parents, but we were very different. I was beginning to understand what Pastor J was talking about when he said we can see an invisible God.

We may not be able to physically see Him, but we see his hand moving in our lives, directing our paths, and allowing us to even be a part of the next day by waking us up. He said God is in control of everything. Nothing catches Him by surprise. We might not understand why He does what He does, but we can be assured that He has everything working for His glory. Just like God told the Israelites through the prophet, Jeremiah in 29:11, *For I know the plans I have for you, declares the Lord, plans for welfare and not for evil, to give you a future and a hope,* God has a plan for His children, that includes us,

If only we could learn to shift our mindsets from ourselves. We are always so quick to say "I did it" instead of saying "God did it". As believers, we must acknowledge His hand in our lives and His will being accomplished through us.

I knew I had not been giving God credit for the things I have or had done in my life. I don't ever remember hearing it put that way. I listened some more and realized there was so much I didn't know about God. I was glad that I had come. There was this feeling of *home* that came over me and I began to cry. I had never felt anything like this before. It was a complete feeling of joy, peace, and calm all at the same time. I touched Marcus's hand and said, "Thank you for inviting me here."

He put his arms around me and hugged me and said, "You are always welcome."

When Pastor J ended his message, the group mingled and caught up with each other. Marcus introduced me to Pastor J.

He was looking intently into my eyes as he spoke to me and said, "Chloe, do you have something you want to talk about?"

I was somewhat stunned at his question because I felt like he was reading my mind. I said, "I do have some questions if you have time."

He said, "It is getting late and we usually go out to eat afterwards. Can you come by tomorrow at 10am? I will be here overseeing the Feed the Homeless mission."

"Tomorrow works for me. I will be here."

The group decided to meet at Applebee's. Walking to Marcus's car, I said, "This was intense. It answered a few questions for me and raised some more. Did you tell Pastor J about me?"

"No, I have never mentioned you to Pastor J."

"I was wondering how he knew I needed to talk."

"Pastor J is spiritual. He sees things that others can't see."

"What does that mean?"

"You will see tomorrow. He is wise beyond his years and he really gets us. I think that is why so many of us keep coming and learning from him. He can speak things we have been thinking, then show us in the Bible the answers to our questions and thoughts. He is going to be able to help you, I am sure of it."

After we all got settled into our seats in Applebee's, we placed our orders and the conversation just took off. Everyone spoke freely about themselves and their lives. One of the guys jokingly said to Marcus, "You finally brought a girl to the class."

Everyone laughed as Marcus was trying to explain that we were just friends. I shared a little about myself and my background and how I knew Marcus. It was fun and I met some nice people. When we were leaving, someone said, "Chloe, I hope you come back next month. It was nice to meet you."

I said, "I plan to be here. It was nice meeting all of you."

It was like we were old friends by the end of the night. When I crawled into bed, I felt exhausted, but more alive and happier than I have ever felt. I could not wait to meet with Pastor J the next day. I had so many questions.

The next morning, I woke up early I was so excited. After putting the coffee pot on, I sat down at my computer and decided to write down my questions. After about thirty minutes, I had over fifty questions. I laughed to myself. Poor Pastor J, he had no idea what was about to happen.

After breakfast, I got dressed and headed over to the church. When I got there, I saw a few of the people from last night standing outside talking. I walked up and said, "Hey, are you all still here?"

They laughed, and one said, "It feels that way. We were just leaving. We came early this morning and packed 300 lunch bags to pass out to the homeless this evening."

"Oh wow, that's awesome. If I had known, I would have come and helped you."

"We are normally here every Saturday morning at 7a.m. You are more than welcome to join us. What are you doing here?"

"I have a meeting with Pastor J at ten."

"Oh okay, I think he is in his office. I will show you where it is. By the way, my name is Tiffany, you are Chloe, right?"

"Yes, I am Chloe, and thanks, I appreciate it."

When we walked into the building, there were people singing "How Great is Our God". They sounded so good I had to stop and listen. I was immediately moved to tears. I said, "They sound great!"

"Yes," smiled Tiffany, "we have some anointed singers here."

We got to Pastor J's door and Tiffany knocked. Pastor J said, "Come in."

"Hi Pastor J! I brought Chloe back to your office. She said you have a meeting with her."

"Yes, I do. Please come in, Chloe."

I said, "Thank you for showing me the way. I will see you next Saturday."

"You are welcome and that would be great!" She closed the door behind her, and I said hello Pastor J.

He answered, "Hi, Chloe! Please have a seat."

We both sat down, and he began talking a little about the church and his background of how he came to be a pastor. I think he was trying to make me feel comfortable, and it worked. He said, "I could sense last night that you had some questions that you wanted to ask but didn't."

"Yes, I have so many, and I am grateful that you agreed to meet with me. I hope you don't mind; I wrote them down so that I would not forget what I wanted to know."

He said, "I don't mind, I think that was a great idea. Lots of people come in and forget why they came in, so making a list works!"

I began to share with Pastor J about my feeling of emptiness and how overwhelming it was at times. He seemed to really understand how I was feeling, and he shared God's word with me and really explained the work of the Holy Spirit and how His job is to keep knocking on our hearts to get our attention.

He continued, "Remember last night when I said in Jeremiah 29:11, that God has a plan for our lives? Well, He uses us here on earth to further His Kingdom and spread His gospel. One of the Holy Spirit's jobs is to create opportunities for us to see God in our lives clearly. Say we are lucky that we got this great job or that we beat cancer. Believers know that it is God's grace in our lives that afforded us these opportunities or outcomes. It's His plan for your life that dictates the opportunities and outcomes. He is always preparing you for something."

We didn't get through all the questions, but I could certainly remembered some situations in my life that could have ended badly, but somehow didn't and I thought I was just lucky. Now, I could connect the dots better by understanding that I had to survive in order to be here having this conversation and learning more about God, Jesus, and the Holy Spirit. Although I still don't know what His plan is for my life, I understand that He has a plan for me and He has been trying to get my attention through the emptiness I have been feeling. We set up another meeting for the following Saturday at ten.

Nodding, I said, "That is perfect because I am going to come and pack some lunch bags next week, so I will already be here."

I left Pastor J's office feeling a lot lighter than when I went in. Driving home, I couldn't stop thinking about everything that Pastor J and I had discussed, and it was like the pieces of a puzzle were starting to come together for me. I said, "Lord, I thank you. I believe I am on the right track."

As I was cleaning up and washing clothes, my mom called.

"Hi Mom! How are you?"

"I am feeling good. How are you?"

"I feel great! I just got home from a meeting with Pastor J, my co-worker Marcus's pastor."

"Why did you meet with him?"

"Well, I went to their singles' Bible study last night and, Mom, it was so good. It was like I heard God speaking directly to me. It was exactly what I needed. The pastor talked about 'seeing an invisible God'. He broke it down so I could really understand what he was talking about. It was like a light bulb went off inside of me."

"That's wonderful! I am so happy to hear this."

"That's not all. Then, when Marcus introduced us, the pastor said to me, 'do you have something you want to talk about'? I thought maybe Marcus had told him about me and how I had been feeling that something was missing, but he had not. So, he set up a meeting with me for today and he was so patient in answering my questions, showing the answers to me in the Word."

"He sounds like a great pastor. Is he married?"

"Oh, Mom, I don't know. I don't want to marry him; I want to know what he knows about God."

"Well, I am just saying he sounds like a good man."

"So, why were you calling? Is everything ok?"

"Yes, I just wanted to remind you that your father and I are going to Houston tomorrow for a few days to visit some friends."

"Okay, thanks for reminding me. I had forgotten about that. What time are you leaving?"

"Around 9a.m."

"When will you be back?"

"On Friday, early in the afternoon."

"Okay, be safe. I love you. Can you send me a text and let me know you got there?"

"Sure, honey. I will. I love you too."

I hung up and got back to cleaning up. Later, Marcus called.

"Hey Chloe, what's up?"

"Hey! Not much. I was just about to watch a movie and relax. What are you doing?"

"Not much, watching the game. I remembered you were meeting with Pastor J this morning. How did it go?"

"Awesome! He was so patient with me. He answered my questions using the scriptures and really opened my eyes to the difference between someone who goes to church and someone who has a relationship with God. I am starting to understand some of the things you have been saying to me all these years. I could not understand why you seemed to always be in church. To me, I didn't think it took all that. If you went on Sunday, why did you have to go on Wednesday and Friday too? I am starting to see it differently now. You weren't going out of obligation to say I went to church on Sunday, and I am good. You were there learning about God and really getting to know Him just like you would with any person you meet. We didn't get to all of my questions, so we have another meeting for next Saturday."

"Oh wow! That is great news, Chloe. I am so glad that Pastor J is opening your eyes spiritually and leading you to

Christ personally. You are going to start to see things differently once you learn to look through the eyes of Jesus. I am so excited for you. Do you want to go to church with me tomorrow? Pastor J is preaching tomorrow."

"Yes, I would love that. What time is church?"

"11am. I can pick you up if you like."

"Sure, what time should I be ready?"

"I will be there at 10:15."

"Okay, great. See you in the morning and thanks for calling, Marcus."

"Cool, see you in the morning."

I watched a movie, ate dinner, and started getting ready for church the following morning. The next day, I woke up excited about what God was going to say today. I got up, got dressed, and Marcus texted to say he was outside. I grabbed my purse and headed out the door.

"Hey, Marcus! You always look so nice in your suits."

He was dressed in a navy-blue suit with silver pinstripes. He had on a gray silk shirt and a navy-blue tie.

"Thanks, Chloe! You look beautiful, as always."

I decided on my blush pink pencil dress with white pearl buttons from my waist to the hem on my right side. The collar of the dress was rounded and white like the pearls. I wore matching pink heels and carried a matching purse.

When we walked into the church, we were met with warm greetings and hugs. I thought, *this is how you are supposed to feel when you walk into a church. It's not like my church, where you are greeted with questions about why you haven't been here.*

It was so warm and inviting. It felt like home. We got into our seats just as the service started. The Praise and Worship team were on fire, and I was on my feet with just about everyone else, praising God. When Pastor J got up, something in me leaped, like I was being called to attention.

He preached about finding God in the hard places in life. He took us to Genesis 50:19–20. It read, *But Joseph said to them, "Do not fear, for am I in the place of God? As for you, you meant evil against me, but God meant it for good, to bring it about that many people should be kept alive, as they are today."*

Pastor J told us the story of Joseph and how his brothers threw him into the pit and left him, then he went to jail for a crime he did not commit. Afterwards, he became the second in command in Egypt. He said, when Joseph said, "Do not fear, for am I in the place of God?" Joseph recognized that his steps had been ordered by God and all the things that happened were part of God's plan for his life.

Joseph could see that he was put in charge of saving his family, along with all of Egypt. Because of that, Joseph was able to forgive his brothers and take care of them after their father died.

Pastor J said sometimes things happen and they seem bad, tragic even, to us. If we could learn to look for God and ask, "What are you trying to teach me, Lord?" He would reveal His purpose in your pain.

Instead, all we want to know is why and why me? We must take the focus off ourselves and look to the Lord. He is all-knowing and He has the answers. We seem to want to wallow in our pity parties, but the Bible never records that Joseph complained about his situation. Clearly, it was a bad situation, but he never asked why.

Pastor J went on to break down our behaviors versus how God wants us to react. It was a good message, and it gave me a few extra questions to add to my list for our meeting on Saturday.

After church, Marcus and I went to brunch at Nine at the National. The buffet seemed to go on for miles with delicacies specialty dishes and drinks. There were so many choices. As we were going through the buffet line, I said, "Everything looks amazing, how do you even choose?"

Marcus laughed and pointed out, "It's a buffet, have one of everything!"

"Of course, so you can laugh as you roll me out of here because I am too stuffed to walk." I selected chicken and waffles with a serving of fruit on the side. Marcus had several pancakes, bacon, sausage, eggs, and fruit on the side. The food was delicious and well presented. I ate so much that I could barely move when it was time to get up to leave.

While enjoying that delicious meal, Marcus asked, "How did you enjoy the service?"

I said, "It felt like home. Everyone was welcoming, and I enjoyed the Praise Team. Pastor J's message was good, but not very relevant to me. I guess I have never felt abandonment or loss like Joseph, so I found it hard to relate, but I understood the message."

Marcus said, "Sometimes the messages are meant to help us in the future. It's not always about things you have already experienced. It is to draw from when something happens in your life that is relatable."

I said, "Okay, I can see that. From that perspective, it is something I need to store in my mind and heart for future use."

"Yes, something like that."

Marcus dropped me off after brunch, and as soon as I got in the door, my phone rang. It was my sister, and she was crying hysterically. All I could make out was "Mom" and "crash".

I said, "I am on my way." Driving, all I could think of was how afraid I was of losing my mom. I can't imagine life without her. How in the world did this happen? How do we go on as a family? She was certainly our glue that held us together. I was terrified.

I got to my sister's house, and she ran into my arms crying uncontrollably and said, "She is gone."

"Who is gone? What are you talking about?"

"Mom! Mom is gone! Oh God, what are we going to do? We must go to University Hospital."

My brain was slowly catching up to what my sister was saying, and I began to lose it. I started shouting, "No, not Mom! Mom and Dad are in Houston." I think I was in shock.

My sister started shaking me. "No, Mom is gone."

We held each other and cried for what seemed like forever. Then, we tried to pull ourselves together. My sister said, "We have to get to the hospital."

I was able to drive us to the hospital somehow. I was just moving motionlessly.

When we got inside the emergency room lobby, my sister's nursing skills kicked in and she asked all the right questions and then we waited for the doctor to come out and tell us what was happening. While we were in the waiting area, a police officer came in and introduced himself. He told us that our parents were driving on Highway

10 when a drunk driver swerved into their lane. Our dad lost control of the car and crashed into a tree.

The officer said, "I am sorry to inform you that your mother died on impact and your father was brought here."

My legs went limp, and the officer had to catch me and place me in the nearest chair. The officer was saying something about the doctor coming soon to update us on our father. My sister and I held each other and cried for what seemed like hours before the doctor came and ushered us into a small conference area and sat us down. He said his name was Dr. Young and he was the attending physician tonight.

All we could do was look at him. Neither one of us spoke for several seconds. Finally, I said, "I'm Chloe and this is my sister Crystal. How is our dad?"

"Your dad has a broken leg, cracked ribs, and a concussion. He has cuts and bruising around his face and arms."

"So, he is going to be okay."

"Yes, I believe he will be."

"Does he know about our mother?"

"I am so sorry for your loss. Yes, he knows about your mother."

"Can we see him?"

"Yes, you can see him in a few minutes. The nurses are getting him situated and hooked up so we can monitor him. One of them will come and get you as soon as they finish."

"Thank you," was all I could get out.

He left the room and I looked at my sister; she was a mess. She asked, "What are we going to do without Mom?"

I said, "I don't know, but we will figure it out together. Can you pull it together for Dad? We are going to see him soon, and I think we need to be strong for him."

She said, "You are right, we need to be strong for Dad." She grabbed a few tissues from the box and began to wipe away her tears.

I stood up and walked around the room to get myself together. When the nurse came in, she said, "Hello, ladies, are you ready to see your dad?"

My sister turned and looked at me, then she looked back and the nurse and said yes. She took my hand, and we walked out, following the nurse. We walked past the nurse's station and down a long hallway. The nurse opened a door and led us into a very large room with several hospital beds behind curtains. We walked past three beds, then the nurse stopped and pulled the curtain back so we could see inside.

My dad looked like he had been in the ring with Rocky. He was all cut and bruised up, bandages were everywhere, and one of his eyes was swollen shut. He was hooked up to machines that were beeping every few seconds and he wore an oxygen mask. My sister immediately went into nurse mode, asking the nurse about his vitals and status. I was grateful she understood what the nurses were saying, so she could relay it to me later in English or non-medical jargon.

I walked over to my dad and touched his hand. He opened his eyes. I said, "Hi, Dad."

In a very weak voice, he said, "Chloe," and started to cry. He said, "I am so sorry I couldn't move out of the way fast enough."

I started crying then, and said, "It's not your fault, Dad." I hugged him as we both cried.

My sister turned and looked at us as she remembered and came out of nurse mode. She started to cry before she reached the bed. She joined us and I put my arm around her too and we just held on tight.

The doctor came in and we pulled apart. My sister wiped the tears from her face and looked at the doctor. She said, "How long do you think my dad will need to be hospitalized?"

The doctor said, "I want to keep him for a day or two and see how he does."

My sister said, "I think that is a good idea. By the way, I am a registered nurse at Dallas Memorial. I have worked in the ER for three years. So, I have a few questions."

She asked the doctor several questions and seemed satisfied with his answers. The doctor turned to my dad and said, "We have you all patched up, sir, and you should be out of here in a few days."

My dad said, "Thank you," as the doctor left the room.

My sister and I hugged our dad again as if we were clinging to him as our lifeline. We finally pulled apart and my father began telling us what happened.

He said, "Your mom and I left about noon, just as we planned. We were laughing, talking, and singing down the road, really excited about our trip. Your mom said, 'Do you think we will ever have grandchildren?' and I said, 'Sure, but no time soon. The girls are too focused on their careers now, just as we taught them. You should be proud of all they have accomplished at such early ages.' 'I am,' she said, 'but I would also love to hear little feet running through the house again.' I said, 'Be patient, you never know what God is going to do.' We got to I-10 in no time at all, then as we were driving along, still singing and laughing, out of nowhere, this car swerves into our lane from the other side of the highway. It happened so quickly; I tried to get out of the way. I lost control of the car and ran straight into a tree. When I woke up, I was here, and your mom was gone."

Tears were streaming down all our faces, and he just kept saying over and over that he was sorry. The nurse came in and said that our dad needed to sleep, so my sister and I gathered our things and kissed him. We said "I love you" and left the room.

My heart felt like it had this gigantic hole in it, and I didn't know how to fix it. I went back to my sister's house, and she asked me to stay, but I just wanted to be alone. So, I went back to my apartment and crawled into bed and cried myself to sleep. When I woke up, I thought it had been a dream. Then, the memory of it all came rushing back.

I reached for my phone to call my sister, but called Marcus instead. "Hey Marcus, this is Chloe."

"How are you?"

"I'm good."

He said, "You sound awful, did you get any sleep last night?"

I began to cry as everything that happened last night poured out and I told Marcus that my mom was dead.

He said, "Oh Chloe, I am so sorry to hear about your mom. Are you okay? Is there anything I can do?"

"No," I said, "I just wanted to ask you a question. Why would God allow this to happen? My mom loved Him, and she lived her life for God. I was learning all these wonderful things about God and now I am not so sure He is wonderful at all."

"Oh Chloe, don't say that. Maybe God wanted to give your mom rest for all her work. You said yourself that she was always at church doing something, right?"

"You know, Marcus, I thought God loved me. Why would He take my mom from me?"

"Chloe, God does love you. Never doubt that. He loves you so much that He gave his son so that you could have eternal life."

"I don't know, Marcus. I am so angry right now that I can't even see straight." Through tears, I said, "My mom was everything to our family. She was the glue that held us together. How can we go on without her? What does God expect us to do without my mom guiding us to Him?"

Very gently Marcus said, "He expects you to pick up her mantle and use what she has taught you to guide others to God."

"I can't do that! I don't even know that much about God."

"I suspect you know more than you think you know. God makes no mistakes, Chloe! It is our job to trust Him, even when we don't understand what is happening."

"Yeah, well, I think I will just go back to working hard. When I was working seven days a week, I didn't feel like this. I was good. I don't like feeling like this."

"Listen, Chloe, don't try to mask your feelings with work."

"I don't know what else to do."

"It is okay to allow your feelings to happen, but don't let them consume you and don't suppress them or cover them up. Look, I am going to put on some clothes, and I will be there in thirty minutes."

"You don't have to do that, Marcus. I'll be okay."

"Are you kidding? I am not letting you go through this alone. I'll be there as soon as I can."

"Okay, bye."

I got out of bed, showered, and got dressed. Then I called my sister to check on her.

"Sounds like I woke you up."

"Yes, I was still asleep."

"How are you doing?"

She said, "I feel numb. It's like my body is refusing to allow me to feel."

"Are you by yourself?"

"No, my friend from work is here with me."

"That's good."

She said, "How about you?"

I said, "My friend, Marcus, is on his way. I called him when I woke up."

"Good, I don't think either of us should be alone right now. I am going to call and check on Dad. I guess we must figure out the funeral arrangements for Mom," my sister choked out.

"Let me know what you need me to do."

"Okay, I will call you after I talk to Dad."

I hung up the phone and my doorbell rang. Marcus came in and hugged me. I started crying again. "I am sorry, I just can't seem to stop crying."

"It's fine, Chloe. You must let the pain out. I talked to Pastor J on my way over here and he wanted to know if it was okay if he came by to see you."

"I don't know, Marcus. I told you I am not feeling God right now. I don't want to be disrespectful or something. It might not be a good idea for Pastor J to see me right now. You know, it really hurts that I didn't get to say goodbye to my mom. I mean, it is like she was here and now she isn't."

As the tears started to flow again, I said, "I don't know how to process that."

"I know, Chloe, that is why I think you should let Pastor J come by. Please don't shut God out."

"I told you, I don't want to hear anything about God right now. Where was He when my mother needed him?"

"Chloe, please don't say that. God is always with His children, you know that."

"Hmph, well right now, I don't see or hear Him. I am not even sure He exists."

Then the doorbell rang. I got up and Marcus said, "That will be Pastor J. When I spoke with him, I told him it would be okay to come see you. I thought you would want to see him."

"Marcus, I am going to kill you for this!" Then I opened the door. "Hello, Pastor J."

"Hello, Chloe. Is it alright if I come in?"

"Yes, sure. Forgive my manners. Please, come in." As I closed the door, I was glaring at Marcus, thinking about how I was going to cut his tongue out for telling Pastor J it was fine for him to come to my house.

I said, "Please, have a seat. Can I get you something to drink? I have water, Pepsi, and fruit punch. I also have coffee and tea if you prefer something hot."

Pastor J said, "Thank you, I would love a cup of coffee."

I started to the kitchen when Marcus jumped up and said, "I'll make the coffee, Chloe. Go have a seat and talk to Pastor J."

I turned from the kitchen and said, "Okay, fine." I didn't even have the energy to argue with Marcus.

So, I sat down and Pastor J said, "Chloe, I am so very sorry to hear about your mom."

As the tears started to flow, I said, "Thank you."

"I want you to know I am here for you. If you need to talk or anything, please know I am available. You know it is important to express what you are feeling and not try to suppress it. God already knows anyway. We can't hide anything from Him."

"Pastor J, no disrespect, but I am not feeling God right now. I was just getting to know Him, or at least I thought I was, then He just allows my mom to die. Why in the world would He do something like that?"

"Chloe, God loves you and He loves your mom. You said she was a believer, right?"

"Yes."

"As much as it hurts because you miss your mom, we have to remember that we all belong to God. She belongs to God and maybe He was ready to give her rest from her work here on earth. I believe that your mom had completed her assignments here on earth and her reward is to be at rest until Christ comes back. That's a great place to be, Chloe. I know it is hard because you miss her and love her. I know you want her here with you. I understand."

Just then, Marcus came back into the room with three coffee mugs and set them on the table. He asked if we wanted sugar or cream as he was headed back into the kitchen to retrieve them. We fixed our coffee and started drinking.

Pastor J picked up where he left off, saying, "I don't know if Marcus told you, but I lost my mom last year. I understand what you are going through. I was very close to my mom. I still pick up my phone to call her sometimes. So, the grief and sorrow are very real, and I am not telling you to not feel those things, but also remember that God's plans are always perfect. He makes no mistakes. Your mom is where we are all trying to get to. Sometimes His will and His purpose don't line up with what we want, but as believers, we have to still believe that He is good."

"Pastor J, this is too much for me. I just can't hear this right now. I am so angry at God. I mean, a drunk driver… really? My mom worked endlessly for that church, giving her money and her time. She texted me scriptures every day. She loved God and her church. I just can't wrap my mind around why He would let this happen to her."

"Chloe, I think you should go to your Bible for your answers and your peace. Read 2 Thessalonians 5:1–9. It may help you to understand things. It helped me when my mom passed."

Angrily I agreed, "Alright, I will read it."

"Once you read it, give me a call and let's talk about it. I don't want to wear my welcome out, but know I am here for you, Chloe."

"Thank you, Pastor J, I appreciate you coming to see me."

He and Marcus stood up and Marcus walked him out. A few minutes later, Marcus returned and said, "Chloe, I am sorry. I thought you would want to talk to Pastor J.

You were so excited about your conversations about God with him."

"You are right, I was excited about my conversations with Pastor J then, but now I don't know if I even believe any of that stuff anymore. I will say, I felt less angry when he was here. He has a very calming effect on me. I didn't know he lost his mom last year. He may have some idea what I am feeling too. So, although I am still mad at you for not asking me first, I don't want to kill you any longer."

"I am glad to hear that. Now, let's go see your dad."

I grabbed my phone and purse, and we headed out the door. We got to the hospital and opened my dad's door, and the room was full. I recognized most of the faces from their church. My sister was there too. People started walking up to me and hugging me and saying how sorry they were about my mom. It seemed like every time someone hugged me, it released my tears, or maybe Marcus was just good at distracting me while we were driving.

He had told me this funny story about one of his dates who started ordering drinks before she even sat down at the table, and by the time they left the restaurant he was practically carrying her to the car. He said her voice was slurring and she was loud and rude to the waitress. He said he was so embarrassed that he wanted to crawl under the table, so he just stopped trying to date women unless they were serious about God.

Finally, after all the hugs and tears, I got to my dad's bedside and hugged him. He looked exhausted and needed to rest. I asked, "Dad, how long have you been awake? You look tired."

One of the church mothers said, "You are right, Chloe. We should go and let your dad get some rest."

So, one by one, they started leaving until it was just my sister, her co-worker, Marcus, and me. Of course, Marcus is comfortable in any setting, so he had introduced himself to everyone and was easily chatting with my sister's co-worker. Then he said, "I am going to find the cafeteria and get coffee. Can I get anyone anything?"

We all said, yes, please. The co-worker said, "I will go with you to help you carry everything."

Once they left, I asked my sister, "What did the doctor say?"

"She said there is no internal bleeding, and his vitals look good, so they are planning to release him tomorrow. He is going to come home with me. Also, we have an appointment at Restland Funeral Home tomorrow at 10am. It is not too far from your house. I will come by and pick you up at 9:40."

"Okay, that sounds good. I can go by the house and get some clothes for dad and bring them to your house. That will be one thing you won't have to do."

"Yes, thank you. That would be helpful. I need to prep my house. I am picking up a wheelchair later today."

We looked back at our dad, and he had fallen asleep. I said, "You can go. I will sit with him for a while."

Marcus came back in and handed me a coffee. He said, "Your co-worker is in the hall on the phone and she has your coffee."

Crystal said, "That's fine. I am leaving anyway, so it was nice to finally meet you, Marcus. Sis, I will see you later this evening."

"Cool, see you later."

Marcus sat down and we started talking quietly about all the things my sister and I had to do for our dad and mom. I said, "Thank you, Marcus, for being there for me today. I don't know if I would have made it without you. If you want to leave, you can. I am going to stay until dad wakes up."

"Then how will you get home? No, I am not going anywhere. Whatever you need, I am here for you today."

So, we talked and laughed and told each other stories about our past. We had been friends for several years, but I didn't know as much about Marcus as I thought I did.

My dad began to stir, and I got up and went to his bedside. I said, "Hi, Dad. Feeling any better?"

"Yes, I am. I really needed that nap. You should have gone home and taken a nap too."

"Don't worry about me, I am fine. I wanted to be here when you woke up in case you needed anything."

I turned the TV on for him and he started watching football and I knew I could leave. He was in his football zone. Marcus was there in the zone with him. I just shook my head and thought, *men, they are all alike*.

I asked, "Dad, is there anything specific that you want me to pick up and drop off at Crystal's for you?"

He said, "You know, our suitcase was in the car with all my toiletries and favorite clothes."

"No worries, I will call Crystal and see where it is, and we will figure out how to get it back. I am going to go now and get your stuff. I will be back later this afternoon. I love you, Dad."

"I love you too, Chloe."

Marcus and I left the room. When I got in the hallway, I called Crystal. She answered right away. "Is Dad okay?"

"Yes, he is. He is watching football. I am on my way to the house. Do you know if they got their suitcase from the car? Dad was asking about their stuff."

"No, I don't know, but the police officer who met us at the hospital gave me his card. I will call him and ask about it."

"Okay, let me know what you find out."

"Chloe, are you going to be okay going to the house alone?"

"I don't know, but you are already doing so much, I need to do something. I should be fine. Plus, Marcus is with me, so I am not alone."

We left the hospital and headed to my mom and dad's house. We went inside and it was eerily quiet. Everything was clean and neat, like my parents would be walking back into the house any minute. I tried not to think too much. I went upstairs and into their room. I noticed a picture of them on the dresser and the tears started flowing.

Long, hard sobs started coming from me as I felt like my heart was being ripped into a million pieces. I could not control myself. I had never felt anything like this. *Oh God, help me, please.*

Marcus put his arms around me and held me for what seemed like forever. I was finally able to regain control of myself and said, "I don't know what happened. It was like I didn't have any control of myself. That was a horrible feeling."

Marcus said, "Grief is not something we can control. We just have to ride it out."

"I have to admit, I am so glad you are here. I'll be right back."

I went into the bathroom and washed my face and tried to pull myself together. I came back out and Marcus was pulling socks from a drawer. I said, "Yes, let's get his stuff. I need to get out of here."

I went to the closet and pulled out a few pairs of pants and some shirts. Marcus had found the underwear and t-shirt drawer and he was pulling out those things. I found a belt and Dad's sneakers. We put all of this on the bed. I left the room and came back with a suitcase to put everything in. Marcus had found some pajamas too.

We quickly put everything in the suitcase. I went into the bathroom to see what I could pack for him. I found everything he needed. My mom was always so good about keeping the house stocked with everything we needed. So, I quickly put his toiletries in the suitcase and closed it up.

Marcus asked, "Did you find everything? Are you ready to go?"

"I did, and yes, I am ready to go."

We left my parent's house and I let out a deep breath. It was as if I had not been breathing the entire time I was in there. "Thank you, Marcus, for coming. I was glad I didn't have to face this alone."

We were standing in the driveway talking when my sister called. "Hi, sis, what's up?"

She said, "I got hold of the police officer, and he said the suitcase should still be inside the car and it has been towed to a parking lot on Irving Street. He emailed me a copy of the police report. He said we would need that to claim the car."

I said, "I will handle that tomorrow. I found everything dad should need at the house."

"Okay, great! Are you okay?"

"I am now. It was much harder than I thought it would be and I am glad Marcus was there with me."

"I am sorry, sis; I should have been there too."

"You have more than enough to do, and I got through it, so no need to be sorry. I am headed to your house now."

Marcus and I got into the car, and twenty minutes later, we pulled up to Crystal's. I rang her doorbell and she let us in. I asked, "How is it going in here? Do you have the room set up for Dad?"

"Yes, I just finished vacuuming and making the bed. I moved a few things around to help him maneuver his wheelchair."

"I will put his clothes in the closet for you."

"Thanks. Marcus, can I get you something to drink?" Crystal asked.

"Yes, a bottle of water would be great, thank you."

She left to get a few bottles of water and I got to work unpacking dad's suitcase. I put everything away and then we sat down and started talking.

"Is there anything else you plan to do in here before Dad gets here?" I asked.

Crystal looked around and said, "No, I think everything is ready."

"So, what do we need for tomorrow?"

"When I pick up dad from the hospital, we are going to go by the bank and get his life insurance policy for Mom and head over to the funeral home."

"Don't forget to pack a small bag for him with a change of clothes for tomorrow."

"I won't."

She started writing down her to do list. I asked, "Have you made any calls? Do you want me to get started on that?"

"I made a few to their church friends and Dad's job."

"I brought Mom's address book with me. I will start making a few calls tonight."

"Okay, that sounds good. Is there anything else you can think of that we need to be doing?"

"No, I don't think so. I am trying to keep a running list so that we don't forget anything or duplicate anything."

"That is a great idea, sis. Do you have any thoughts about the funeral?"

"I think we should discuss that after I pick up Dad from the hospital. He gets to make those decisions. Oh, that's right. I have a list of things he must do too, just in case he needs help."

"Thank God I have you. You are really on it, sis! I remember as a kid you always had a list. You planned everything. You would even write out a grocery list for Mom to carry to the store."

She laughed, "I know. Mom loved to get my list and take it with her. She started asking for it. She was a great mom! She had us try everything to see if it was something we loved and were good at. She wanted to celebrate everything, even when we got one basketball game shot. She was ready to go get pizza and talk about how awesome the shot was. She would make us feel like we were the stars of the team no matter how bad we sucked at the game."

Marcus laughed, saying, "I would have loved to see you playing basketball. I can't even imagine that."

I rolled my eyes at him and said, "What, you don't think I had game? You would have been impressed with my skills." We all laughed, imagining what that would look like.

"What about the arts and crafts?" Crystal thought aloud. "Mom could make anything. She made our costumes and even some of our sports uniforms. She was our biggest cheerleader. She believed we could do anything, so we believed it too."

"Well," I yawned, "I am wiped out. Is your co-worker coming back to stay with you tonight?"

"Yes, she should be here any minute. Her shift ended about an hour ago."

"Great! I am exhausted. Marcus, I think we should go. I am sure we have bored you enough with our old stories."

"Bored? Not at all. I have lots of ammunition to keep you in line at work."

"OMG let's go!"

Right as we were getting up to leave, Crystal's co-worker knocked on the door. I answered the door and let her in. We said our hellos and I said, "See you in the morning, Crystal."

"Good night, you two."

Marcus said goodnight and we closed the door. Walking to the car, Marcus said, "You really have a great family."

I smiled. "Thanks. I guess I do. I never really thought about it. Usually my mom or my sister are complaining about something I am not doing or didn't do. At least, that is how it feels to me. You see how organized my sister is? She is always like that. She never forgets anything, and she is always on time and eager to help. Me, on the other hand, I am always running late. I forget about dinners and birthdays, I miss appointments, and I always seem to be rushing in or out. Crystal is definitely the favorite if there was choosing happening. She makes everything seem effortless."

We got back to my house and out of the car. I said, "Marcus, you don't have to stay with me."

He said, "I know, but I am. I have a bag in the trunk. I told you I am here for you and you are stuck with me." He got his bag, and we walked to my door. We laughed, talking about some of our co-workers and what they would be saying about him spending the night at my house. We would definitely be the talk of the office, just scandalous!

We were still laughing as I got the guest room ready for him. "Marcus, are you hungry? I feel like we didn't eat much today. Would you like a sandwich? Sorry, I don't really have much else. I need to go grocery shopping."

"I told you my sister would have stopped by and picked up dinner for us."

"I am more of a fly by the seat of my pants type of girl."

He laughed and said, "Yes, I will take a sandwich and you are anything but a fly by the seat kind of girl! You are more of a codes and algorithms type of girl."

"That is oh so true! When I see patterns and equations, I am in my element, but plans, lists, and schedules are hard for me to follow. I think it drives my family crazy. Oh well, we are all different."

"Yes," Marcus said, "made uniquely by God."

I went into the kitchen and made us a couple of sandwiches with chips and bottles of water and dinner was served. "You know, I haven't opened my laptop all day. I should probably at least check my emails."

"You don't have to. I called Mr. Thomas and told him about your parents, he was very understanding. He told me to tell you that he was very sorry to hear about your mother and if there was anything you needed, to please let him know. He immediately looked into your projects and either put them on hold or reassigned them if they were time sensitive. You don't need to worry about work right now."

"Thank you so much, Marcus."

We finished our sandwiches and I put the dishes in the dishwasher. Marcus was on his laptop, probably catching up on his own work that he missed today because of me. I said, "Don't stay up too late. I am going to bed. I am exhausted."

He said, "I won't. Have a good night's sleep, Chloe."

"You too, Marcus. Thanks again for everything. See you in the morning."

I went in my room, closed the door, and got myself ready for bed. I crawled into bed, and was fast asleep before my head hit the pillow. The next morning, I woke up rested, but dreading the day ahead. I showered and dressed in a pair of black jeans with a tan and black tee shirt and a tan blazer. I came out of my room and Marcus was already dressed in jeans and a light blue polo shirt, drinking a cup of coffee and looking at his laptop.

He looked up and said, "Good morning, Chloe. How did you sleep?"

"Good morning, Marcus. I slept well. How about you?"

"I slept well also. That mattress is amazing! I had to look to see the brand."

"It is practically brand new. I hardly ever have guests, so it has only been used maybe twice before last night."

"All I know is I slept well, and at home I never sleep like that. So, I am getting a new mattress. Do you want breakfast?"

"No, I don't think I can eat before our appointment at the funeral home. I am feeling nervous. I will just have coffee, thanks."

"Okay, well we better be on our way."

We both finished our coffees and I put the cups in the dishwasher, then we grabbed our stuff and left. "Traffic is heavy out here," I said. "Shouldn't these people be at work?"

"Normally we wouldn't see this because we would already be at work."

We started talking about a project that Marcus was working on. "I have tried every code I can think of," he said. "Nothing is working."

"I will look at it when we get back to the apartment and see if I can figure it out."

"That would be great because I am ready to scrap it."

We finally got to the funeral home. Of course, my sister and dad were already there. I said, "See? Even when I leave early, I am always the last to show up."

Marcus laughed and said, "It's not a competition, Chloe!"

"I know that. I am just saying that it is always like this."

"You do know we are on time; we are not late, right?"

"I know, but why am I always last?"

"Remember, not a competition."

"Right…"

We got out of the car and headed over to my sister's car. Marcus helped my dad out of the car and got him into his wheelchair and we went inside. The funeral director took us into his office right away. We all sat down at a large conference table with a box of tissues in the middle of the table. He pulled out a few books with caskets in several styles and colors in them. He handed my dad a brochure with their different services, along with the prices.

My dad looked at the different choices and made the selection. He and my sister discussed casket colors, and I just sat there thinking I couldn't breathe. It was too much.

I stood up and said, "Excuse me, where is your restroom?" I left the room, found the restroom, and soon as I closed the door, I bent over trying to catch my breath. I felt like I had been running a marathon. Everything started to spin, and I fell on the floor. I thought I was going to die.

My sister came in and she put her arms around me and held me tight. I finally began to calm down and breathe normally again. She said, "You had a panic attack."

I said, "I was so sure I was dying. I have never felt anything like that before."

She checked my pulse, and it was back to normal. We got off the floor and went back into the conference room. My dad was shaking hands with the funeral director, and said, "Chloe are you okay?"

"Yes, Dad, I am fine."

"We are all done. We can go to the florist now."

We all thanked the funeral director and headed back to the lobby. Marcus stood up and said, "That was quick. Are you all done?"

"Yep, all done," I said.

He helped my dad back into my sister's car and we got in the back of her car with them and went to the florist. After picking out the flowers, we all went to lunch. My dad looked sad, but strong. My sister was handling all the details and I was just a mess.

When we got back to Marcus' car, we said our goodbyes and I asked Marcus if he would take me home because I needed to be alone. He asked, "Are you sure? I really don't want to leave you like this."

"I will be fine. I just need time to think and process. You have been amazing, and I appreciate everything you have done. I promise to call you later."

So, he dropped me off and I went into my apartment and sat down on the couch. I opened my laptop and started writing down what I was feeling. I felt lost and sad. I felt uncertain and scared. I really wanted to talk to my mom, but she was no longer here for me to talk too. Now, I was angry and couldn't believe God would take my mom from me. Why my mom? Why now?

The tears would not stop, and the anger would not go away. It was suffocating me. I stood up and paced the floor wanting to scream. The anger was like a covered pot on the stove with water boiling up to the top needing to get out and escape the heat. My emotions were out of control. I was trying to calm down, but nothing helped.

Then, my phone rang, and it was Pastor J. *OMG. Not now, I don't want to talk to him.* But something urged me to answer the phone.

"Hello?"

"Hi Chloe, this is Pastor J. How are you?"

"I am doing ok. How are you?"

"I was praying and you kept coming to my mind. The Spirit was urging me to call you. Are you sure you are okay?"

"Look, Pastor J, I don't really want to hear anything about the Spirit or God right now. I feel like I am about to explode, and I don't want you to be the target, so can I call you later?"

"Chloe, I know you are upset, and you feel like you need someone to blame. I get it, but blaming God is never the answer. God is love. We don't always understand His ways and thoughts, but that doesn't change who He is. This tragic accident is awful, and it can have all kinds of repercussions for many people, but God always has a plan, and He knows our future. I know you think you don't want to hear this, but His word is what is going to bring you comfort. Jeremiah 29:11 says, *'For I know the plans I have for you, declares the Lord, plans for welfare and not for evil, to give you a future and a hope'.*

"Your mom loved the Lord, and she ran her race well. Do you think she would want to see you going backward, pulling away from God or running toward Him, drawing even closer? Chloe, you told me you felt like something was missing, like you were being drawn to Christ. You were right at the door about to open it and let Christ in and then this tragic accident happens. You know the enemy would want you to walk away from the door and never look back, but I believe you are stronger than the enemy, Chloe.

"You can defeat Him right now by opening up the word of God and allowing God to wrap His word around you and comfort your broken heart. He is the only one who can heal your heart. Let Him in Chloe, right now. In the midst of your pain, let Him in."

It was like the dam broke and the water came gushing through and over the rocks. I screamed out for God, and I could feel Him putting me back together like a puzzle, adding that missing piece, which was Jesus. I have never felt anything like it.

A peace came over me and settled so firmly around me like a warm blanket, feeling secure and safe. Then I said, "Lord, I love You. Thank You for saving me."

Pastor J said, "Hallelujah! You did it, Chloe. Welcome to the family."

I opened my Bible app and said, "What was that scripture you read in Jeremiah?"

Pastor J said, "Jeremiah 29:11."

I found it and read it out loud. Pastor J began to minister to me through the word of God and the anger left and there was only peace. I was still sad. I missed my mother beyond words, but what I gained in Christ gave me the strength to handle it.

At my mom's funeral, God gave me the strength to get up and speak about her love for God and how everything she did centered around Him. For years, I didn't understand it. I felt like she was missing out on so much of life because of church, but now I saw that I was the one missing out. It wasn't church that she was following, it was God, and He has everything I need and so much more.

I am so grateful that the Spirit of God kept trying to get in and that I finally opened the door wide and allowed full access. He was the missing piece and now I feel whole and complete in Him.

After a week of helping my sister with our dad, getting our mom's estate business going, and figuring out schedules since dad was going to be in a cast for another several weeks, it was time to go back to work.

I checked my emails and made a list of what I would handle first when I got in tomorrow. Then, my phone rang and it was Josh.

"Hi Josh," I said. "How are you?"

"I am great. I was so sorry to hear about your mom. How are you doing?"

"It is very different, but I am managing. I am going back to work tomorrow."

"Really? I thought you would be off another few weeks.""

I'd rather not sit around here and think about her. Working will help me to keep my mind focused."

"I definitely understand that."

"So, what's new with you? Have you made a decision about the job offer? Are you leaving Dallas?"

"Yes, I am. I thought about what you said and decided to take your advice. I asked Janet to go with me and she said yes! I am having a going away party in two weeks and I am going to ask Janet to marry me."

I was speechless. "Wow" was all I could get out. "I certainly didn't see that coming. Congratulations on all of that! I am very happy for you both."

"Thank you, Chloe, that really means a lot to me. Our last conversation really put things into perspective for me. I value our friendship more than you know. I hope we can keep in touch."

"Absolutely we will stay in touch. All the best to you in your new job and life. Well, let me get ready for my first day back to work."

"I will talk to you soon."

"Take care and tell Janet I said congratulations!"

"I will."

"Talk to you later, Chloe!"

"Bye."

After hanging up the phone, I started getting ready for work. I thought to myself, if I was Janet, would I have said yes to going to San Francisco with Josh? No, I would not have given up my job and moved away from my family. I liked Josh, but not that much. Good for them!

It was Monday morning, and I reflected on life as I was returning to work. I would rather be focusing on work than my mom being gone. I had learned so much since meeting Pastor J, and I understand that God's will trumps my feelings, I definitely get that, but I miss my mom so much and sitting here in my apartment is not helping me. I need something else to think about.

Selene was another issue that had been plaguing my thoughts. I spoke with Pastor J about her, and I have prayed for her and our relationship. Only God knows if our relationship will weather this storm.

I am learning to put my faith in God and allowing Him to lead and guide me. Pastor J has been so helpful in teaching me about God, answering my questions, and showing me in the scriptures where to find my answers. I am grateful that God put him in my life to help me stay grounded in God even during one of the most difficult storms I have faced.

I am so blessed to finally feel whole. I no longer feel like something is missing. God filled that void with the Holy Spirit, and everything clicked into place. Although I am sure I will continue to have difficult times in my life, I now am confident about relying on the Holy Spirit to help me navigate through it. I truly believe that with God all things are possible!

Made in the USA
Middletown, DE
20 October 2023